Dearest Barrett, Whitney + Jack ♡

Jill Kargman & Sadie Kargman

Pirates & Princesses

ILLUSTRATED BY **Christine Davenier**

enjoy!

xoxo

Jill

DUTTON CHILDREN'S BOOKS
an imprint of Penguin Group (USA) Inc.

Dedicated with love to The Episcopal School in the City of New York—
a warm, special place where pirates and princesses play together—and
to the Chapin School, which fosters Sadie's love of storytelling every day.
—J & S K

Pour Leo et pour Louis, les pirates de Marseille, et Paola, la princesse de l'Estaque!
—C D

DUTTON CHILDREN'S BOOKS • A division of Penguin Young Readers Group
Published by the Penguin Group • Penguin Group (USA) Inc., 375 Hudson Street, New York, New York 10014, U.S.A.
Penguin Group (Canada), 90 Eglinton Avenue East, Suite 700, Toronto, Ontario, Canada M4P 2Y3 (a division of Pearson Penguin Canada Inc.)
Penguin Books Ltd, 80 Strand, London WC2R 0RL, England
Penguin Ireland, 25 St Stephen's Green, Dublin 2, Ireland (a division of Penguin Books Ltd)
Penguin Group (Australia), 250 Camberwell Road, Camberwell, Victoria 3124, Australia (a division of Pearson Australia Group Pty Ltd)
Penguin Books India Pvt Ltd, 11 Community Centre, Panchsheel Park, New Delhi - 110 017, India
Penguin Group (NZ), 67 Apollo Drive, Rosedale, Auckland 0632, New Zealand (a division of Pearson New Zealand Ltd)
Penguin Books (South Africa) (Pty) Ltd, 24 Sturdee Avenue, Rosebank, Johannesburg 2196, South Africa
Penguin Books Ltd, Registered Offices: 80 Strand, London WC2R 0RL, England

Text copyright © 2011 by Jill and Sadie Kargman

Illustrations copyright © 2011 by Christine Davenier

Library of Congress Cataloging-in-Publication Data

Kargman, Jill, date.
Pirates & Princesses / by Jill Kargman & Sadie Kargman ; illustrated
by Christine Davenier.—1st ed.
p. cm.
Summary: Ivy and Fletch have been best friends since they were born but now, at age five, the boys
in their kindergarten play Pirates at recess while the girls play Princesses, and the duo is split apart.
ISBN 978-0-525-42229-7 (hardcover : alk. paper)
[1. Best friends—Fiction. 2. Friendship—Fiction. 3. Sex
role—Fiction. 4. Play—Fiction. 5. Kindergarten—Fiction.
6. Schools—Fiction.] I. Kargman, Sadie. II. Davenier, Christine, ill.
III. Title. IV. Title: Pirates and Princesses.
PZ7.K1343Pir 2011
E—dc22   2011005191

Published in the United States by Dutton Children's Books,
a division of Penguin Young Readers Group
345 Hudson Street, New York, New York 10014
www.penguin.com/youngreaders

Designed by Irene Vandervoort • Manufactured in Singapore • First Edition

10 9 8 7 6 5 4 3 2 1

Ivy and Fletch had known each other their entire lives.

That's five whole years, people!

Their mommies had been pregnant at the same time. They went shopping together, and bought strollers and cribs and bottles and pacifiers and bouncy chairs and burp cloths and car seats and swings. There was lots of stuff. Stuff stuff stuff. And more stuff.

The babies arrived one day apart. And then the mommies got together so the babies could play side by side. There were squeaky toys and rattling toys and musical toys and furry toys and fluffy toys and toys with googly eyes.

Mostly though, Ivy and Fletch just stared at each other and drooled a lot.

The babies grew and grew. They ate mushy food, then small food, then cut-up food, then real food.

Gurgles turned to babbles turned to words turned to sentences (even if the mommies couldn't understand them at first).

Sitting turned to crawling

turned to walking-like-a-zombie

turned to running.

Slow down, kiddos!

In no time at all, Ivy and Fletch went to preschool. Some kids cried when their parents dropped them off, but Ivy and Fletch skipped off happily.

While the others fought over crayons and costumes and trucks and puzzles and books, Ivy and Fletch shared nicely. (Hey, they'd been sharing since they were wearing onesies in the drooly days.)

During outside time, snack time, story time, and nap time, the two were best pals. They did everything together.

And then came kindergarten, where the big kids go. Ivy and
Fletch were excited to find their cubbies right next to each other,
just like in preschool! But they soon realized this kindergarten
place was . . . different.

Instead of sitting on the floor, they sat at tables. Instead of painting with their fingers, they painted with brushes. And nap time? That was gone, baby, gone.

But there was a super new thing called RECESS.

When the recess bell rang, the kids burst onto the playground. Ivy and Fletch ran to the swings, where they played a game they invented called Twisty Cakes. One friend twisted the other's swing around and around and then let go, making the other spin, spin, spin.

But while Ivy and Fletch played on the swings together, all of the other girls were with the girls and the boys were with the boys.

The next day, Hugh, Will, Harry, and Carter approached Fletch during recess. "Ahoy, matey!" they said. "The jungle gym is our pirate ship! Come join our pirate team."

Sasha, Eloise, Nancy, and Marina went up to Ivy and said, "Come to the playhouse! It's our palace. We are the princess team!"

The pirates brought Fletch back to their ship. They climbed up to the top tower. "What's the pirate password?" Will asked Fletch.

"I don't know," Fletch said with a shrug.

"Okay, I'll tell you, but it's TOP SECRET. You can't tell any of the girls. It's *ARRGH!*"

The pirates talked about superheroes and dinosaurs and cupcakes. They jousted and walked the plank and fought off a pack of flying sea dragons.

"Ivy," Sasha whispered. "The special password to our princess palace is TIARA."

The girls talked about ballet and fairies and kitty cats and cupcakes. They pirouetted and braided hair and held ball-gown fashion shows.

Ivy and Fletch were having so much fun with their new pirate and
princess posses that they were starting to forget each other . . . almost.
As the pirates made a treasure chest out of leaves and branches,
Marina said, "Those grody boys are playing in the dirt. Ewww!"

And while the princesses practiced ballet steps, Will said, "Girls are
so silly. They look like a bunch of birds!"
Then, one day, the pirates decided to do what pirates do . . .

RAID!

"You know what this means, princesses," said Eloise as the pirates charged the palace. "WAR!"
The pirates chased the princesses. The princesses chased the pirates.

And then the pirates caught themselves a royal hostage: PRINCESS IVY!

Ivy didn't mind at first.

But then the boys made a wall around her. The other princesses tried
to rescue her, but they couldn't break through.

Fletch thought it was great fun—until he saw Ivy's face.

He knew that look, even from the diaper days: She was scared.

"Let her out of the jail!" Fletch demanded, pulling Ivy through the wall of boys.

"Hey, are you a pirate or not?" demanded Carter.

"C'mon, Ivy," said Nancy, reaching for Ivy's hand. "You don't want to be near those stinky pirates."

Ivy and Fletch looked at each other.

Ivy linked her arm with Fletch's. "He's my friend," she said.

All of the pirates and princesses gasped.

"I'm sorry I left you for the pirates," Fletch said. "I like those guys, but I've known you my whole life!"

Ivy agreed. "I liked being a princess, but I'm glad we can play stuff like Twisty Cakes again."

Ivy stopped in her tracks. "That gives me an idea!" she said excitedly. Then she yelled as loud as any pirate could into the gusty winds: "All pirates and princesses, come to the swing set!"

Together, Ivy and Fletch taught the kids how to play Twisty Cakes. The kids twirled and giggled and yelled *WHEEEE!* and got dizzy and took turns doing it again and again.

Little by little, other games followed, like Leaping Lizards, Run from Hot Lava, and Pin the Tail on Miss Quackenbush. Soon the playhouse was just a playhouse, and the jungle gym was just a jungle gym. And instead of being growly captains and royal highnesses, they were just Will and Eloise and Sasha and Hugh and Nancy and Carter and Marina and Harry and Ivy and Fletch.

They still played pirates and princesses for old times' sake, but there were no secret passwords and anyone was allowed on either team.

After all, there's a little pirate and princess in all of us. And whether you're as fierce and rowdy as the stormy seas or prefer a peaceful princess palace, one of the best pirates' treasures is a cupcake with friends.